THE FIVE
OF US

Quentin Blake

THE FIVE OF US

OF US

Tate Publishing

For Loopy and Corky

Once, not very long ago, and not very far from here,
there were five friends. Their names were

Angie,

Ollie,

Simona,

Mario

and Eric.

They were all fantastic.

Angie could see a sparrow sitting
on top of a statue five miles away.
She was amazing.

Ollie could hear it sneeze.
He was amazing.

Simona and Mario were so strong
they could lift anything you could think of.
They were amazing.

Eric was just as amazing,
but you will find out how later on.

On the day of the outing
they all set off in the yellow bus.

Big Eddie was driving.

Soon they were in the country.

Angie could see a sheepdog
sitting on a wall miles away.

Ollie could
hear it bark.

WUF
WUF

Simona and Mario lifted Eric up
so that he could look out of the top of the bus.

He said, 'Erm … erm.'

They drove further and further up
into the hills, until they found
a good place to eat their sandwiches.

They had banana sandwiches,
egg and tomato sandwiches,
and cheese and pickle sandwiches.

Angie said, 'I love
banana sandwiches.'

Ollie said, 'Cheese and pickle
are my best.'

Simona said, 'Yum-yum.'

Mario said, 'I could eat
ten of each of them.'

Eric said, 'Erm … erm.'

But when they had finished
    their sandwiches and were
having a little rest,
    Big Eddie said, 'I think
I feel a bit peculiar.'

Then he went green.

Then he went white.

And then he fainted clean away
— THUD.

'Perhaps it was the sandwiches,'
said Mario.

'Poor Eddie,' said Simona.

'At least I can hear his heart
beating,' said Ollie.

'We must find somewhere where
he can be looked after,' said Angie.

Eric said, 'Erm … erm.'

And so they set off to look for help.

They kept on for a long while.

Then Angie said,
'I can see some people.'

And Ollie said,
'I can hear them talking.
They can help us.'

And then suddenly they came
to the banks of a river.

'What do we do now?' said Angie.

And then Eric walked to the edge
    of the river and said, 'Erm ... erm ... '

P!

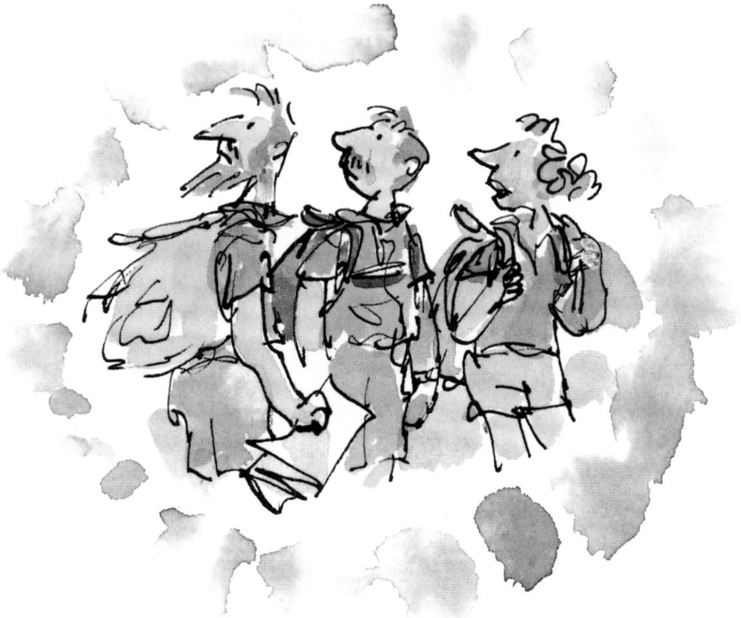

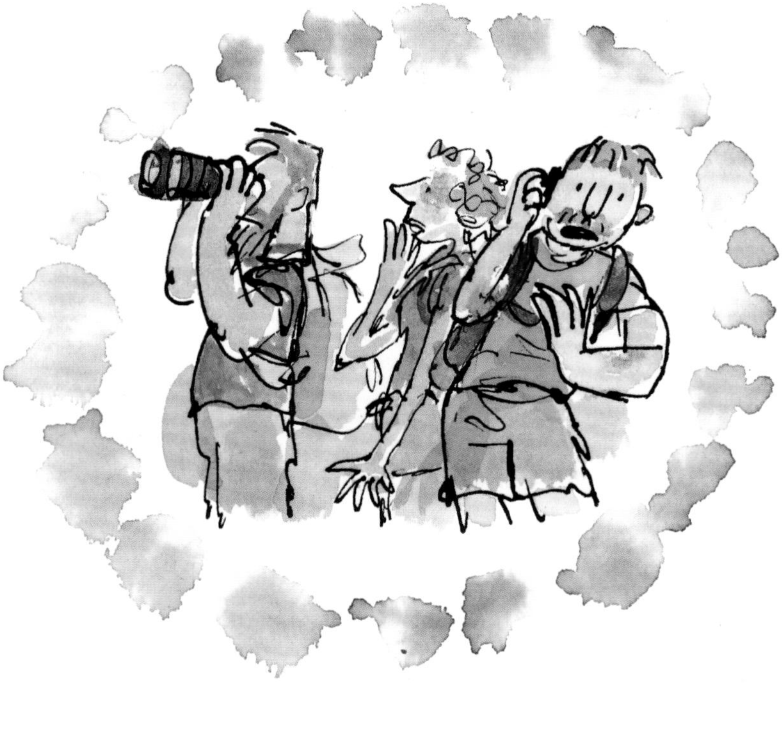

In what seemed like no time at all

Angie could see it coming

Ollie could hear it coming

And then there it was —

HELICOPTER RESCUE !

LK4790
PXQZ

Angie and Ollie and
Eric and Simona and Mario
and Big Eddie
were all hauled up safely.

The next day they
went to see Big Eddie
in hospital.

He was feeling much better, and he said,
'What a rescue! My goodness, I don't know what
I would have done without you.'

And Eric said, 'Erm … erm …

Just leave it to the Fantastic Five!'

First published 2014 by order of the Tate Trustees
by Tate Publishing, a division of Tate Enterprises Ltd,
Millbank, London SW1P 4RG
www.tate.org.uk/publishing

Text and artwork © Quentin Blake 2014

A catalogue record for this book is available
from the British Library
ISBN 978 1 84976 304 2

Distributed in the United States and Canada
by ABRAMS, New York
Library of Congress Control Number applied for

Designed by Atelier Works
Colour reproduction by DL Imaging, London
Printed by Toppan Leefung in China